Augustus et son Sourire

Augustus and his Smile

Text and Illustrations copyright © Catherine Rayner 2006
Catherine Raynor has asserted her right to be identified as the author and
illustrator of this work under the Copyright, Designs and Patents Act, 1988
Dual language copyright © Mantra Lingua 2008
Printed in Norwich,UK 2M300313PB04131747

Mantra Lingua
303 Ballards Lane, London N12 8NP
www.mantralingua.com

First published in UK
by Little Tiger Press 2006
This edition published 2013

A CIP catalogue record for this book
is available from the British Library

Audio copyright ©
Mantra Lingua 2008

Thank you, Mum, Brian and Colin - C R

ABOUT THIS BOOK

From Annie Apple and Bouncy Ben to the Yo-yo Man
and Zig-Zag Zebra, you'll find all the LETTERLAND characters
as well as more than 400 first words in the
LETTERLAND PICTURE DICTIONARY.

On every page there's a useful 'Find the Word List'.
It includes all the words that appear in the picture, whether they
are printed labels or writing on an explorer's map or the
front of Bouncy Ben's book.

Use the list for quick reference or for simple word recognition games.
In the case of vowels, we list short and long vowel sounds separately.

You'll also find some suggested activities, designed to
stimulate the young reader's imagination. They'll help encourage
children to count caterpillars with Clever Cat or help the
Hairy Hat Man find a hidden hippo.

Each page includes lots more opportunities for discussion;
because the more you look, the more you'll discover to talk about.

What's the Doctor doing in the deckchair? He's dozing!
Maybe he's even dreaming about dragons!

Every time you open this book you'll discover something new,
because LETTERLAND makes learning fun.

LETTERLAND
Picture Dictionary

Devised and written by Richard Carlisle

Educational Editor: Lyn Wendon

LETTERLAND
Direct

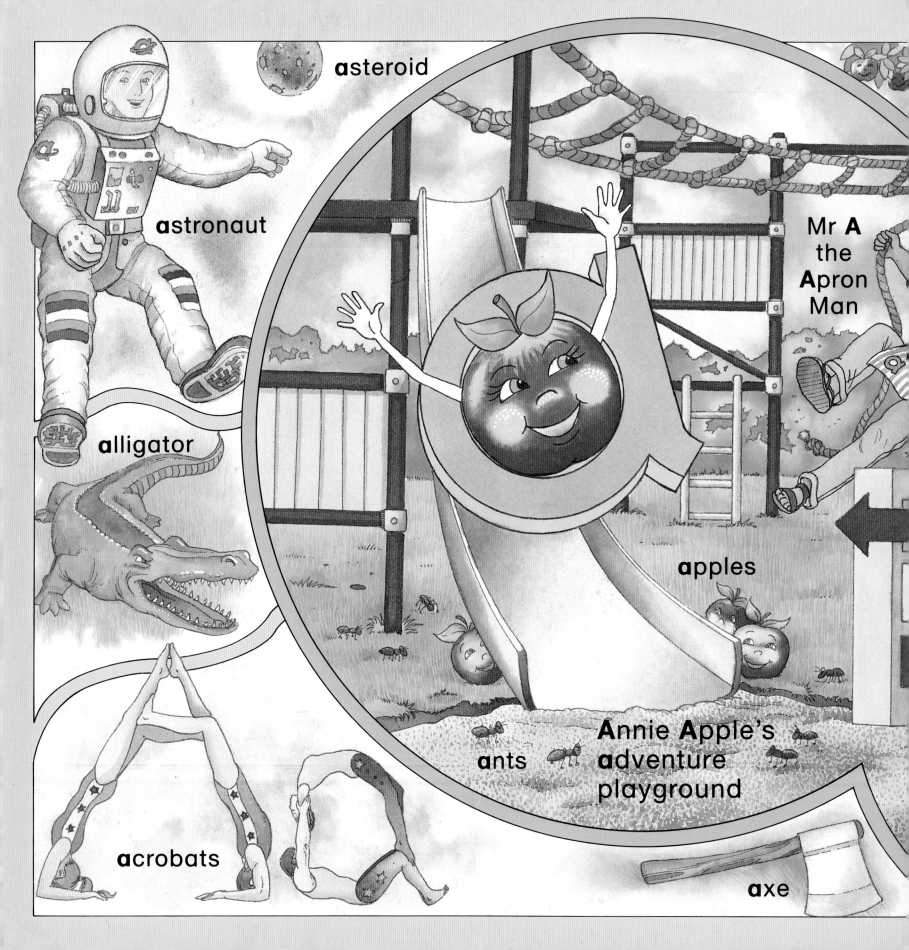

asteroid

astronaut

alligator

acrobats

Mr **A**
the
Apron
Man

apples

ants

Annie **A**pple's
adventure
playground

axe

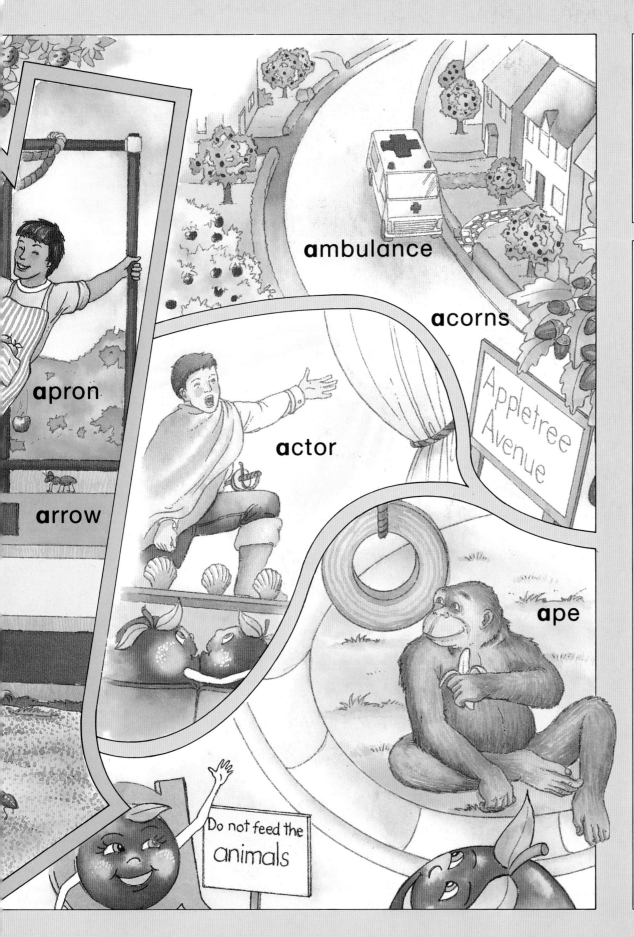

apron

arrow

ambulance

acorns

actor

Appletree Avenue

ape

Do not feed the animals

Find the word

acrobats	**a**pples
actor	**A**ppletree
adventure	**a**rrow
alligator	**a**steroid
ambulance	
animals	**a**stronaut
Annie	**A**venue
ants	**a**xe
Apple	

Mr **A**

acorns	**a**pron
ape	

Activities

Add up all the apples.

Add up all the ants.

Find an angry animal.

bat

balloon

bus

bus stop

butterfly

Bouncy **B**en
on the **b**each

book

beetle

branch

blue
birds

ball

bird **b**ath

bees

bear

breakfast in **b**ed

blanket

boat

bottle

butter

baked **b**eans

brown **b**read

bridge

bicycle

BANG!

Find the word

baked	**B**irthday
ball	**b**lanket
balloon	**B**LOB
BANG!	**b**lue
bat	**b**oat
bath	**b**ook
beach	**b**ottle
beans	**B**ouncy
bear	**b**ranch
bed	**b**read
bees	**b**reakfast
beetle	**b**ridge
Ben	**b**rown
bicycle	**b**us
BIG	**b**us stop
bird	**b**utter
birds	**b**utterfly

Activities

Count all the bees.

Find something buried on the beach.

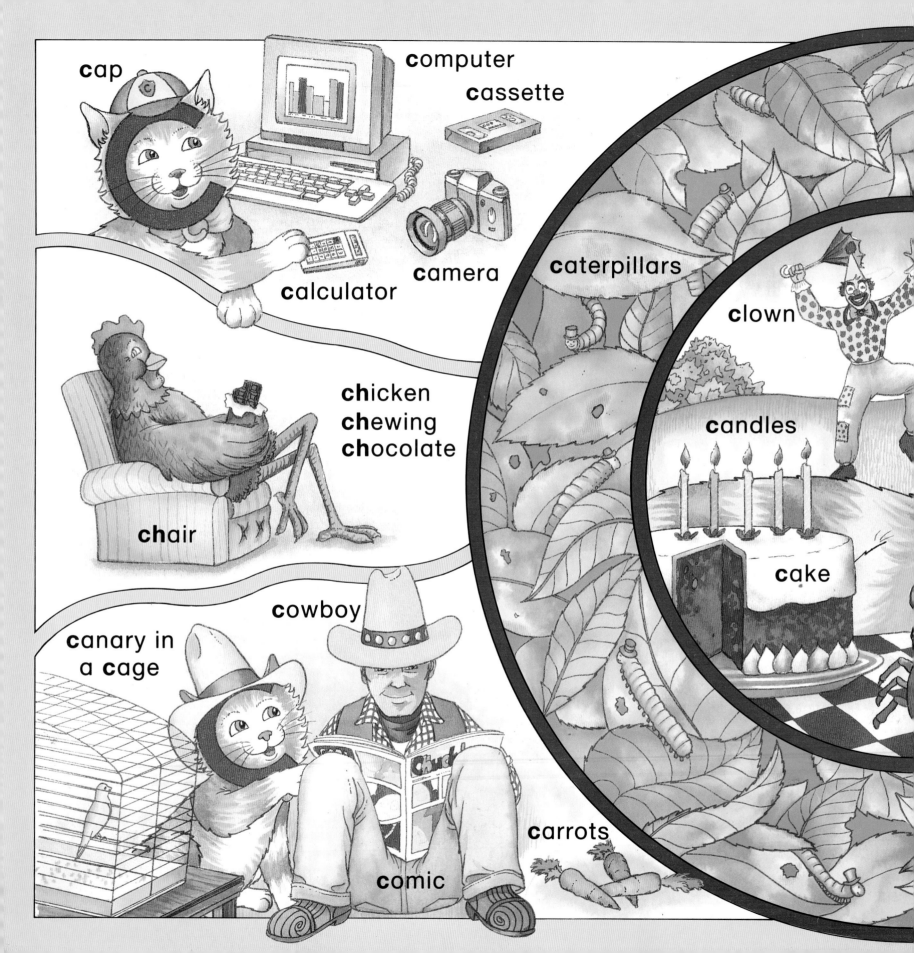

cap

computer

cassette

camera

calculator

caterpillars

clown

candles

chicken
chewing
chocolate

chair

cake

cowboy

canary in
a **c**age

carrots

comic

clock covered in cobwebs

crow

Clever Cat's picnic

church

camel

claws

crab

crane

crate

car

Find the word

cage	chocolate
cake	church
calculator	Clever
camel	claws
camera	clock
canary	clown
candles	cobwebs
cap	comic
car	computer
carrots	covered
cassette	cowboy
Cat	crab
caterpillars	
chair	crane
chewing	crate
chicken	crow

Activities

Find all the caterpillars.

Count the candles on Clever Cat's cake.

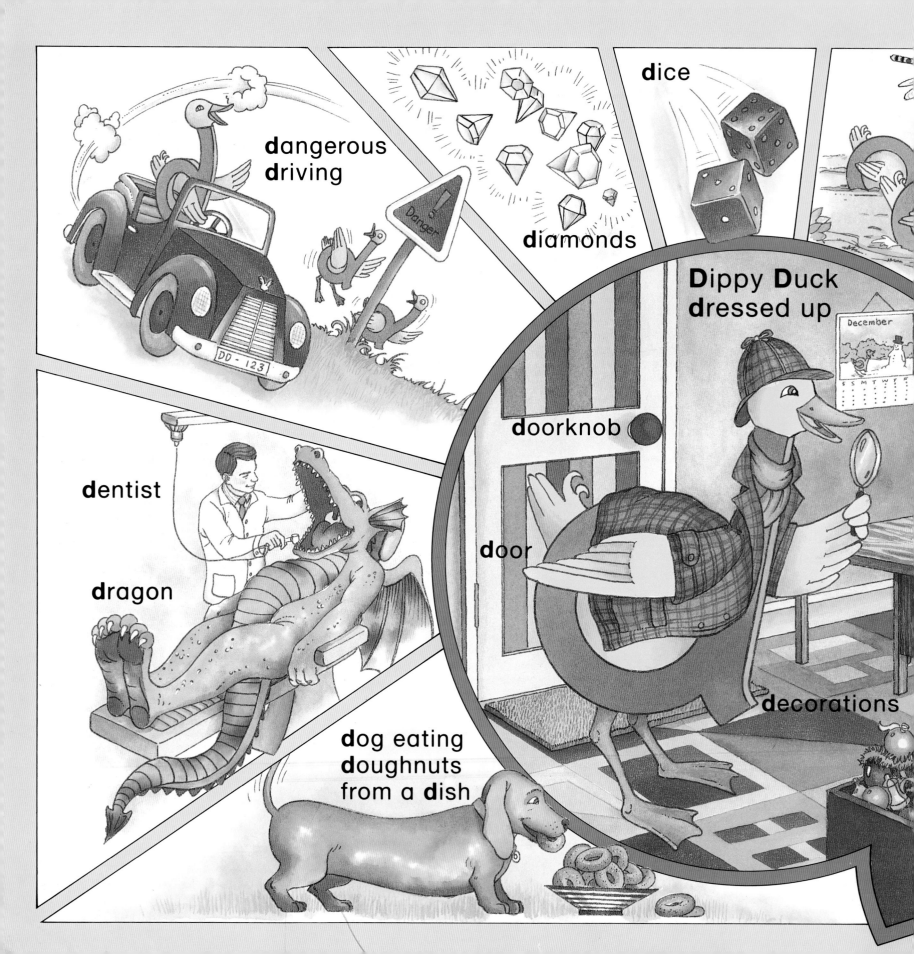

daffodils

dartboard

Doctor in a **d**eckchair

DO NOT DISTURB

desk

doll

diving dolphins

drum

drumsticks

Which **d**oor is **d**ifferent?

Dd

Find the word

daffodils	**D**O
Danger!	**D**octor
dangerous	
dartboard	**d**og
December	**d**oll
deckchair	**d**olphins
decorations	
dentist	**d**oor
desk	**d**oorknob
diamonds	**d**oughnuts
dice	**d**ragon
different	**d**ressed
Dippy	**d**riving
dish	**d**rum
DISTURB	**d**rumsticks
diving	**D**uck

Activities

Add up the dots on the dice.

Find the dove.

Count the ducks.

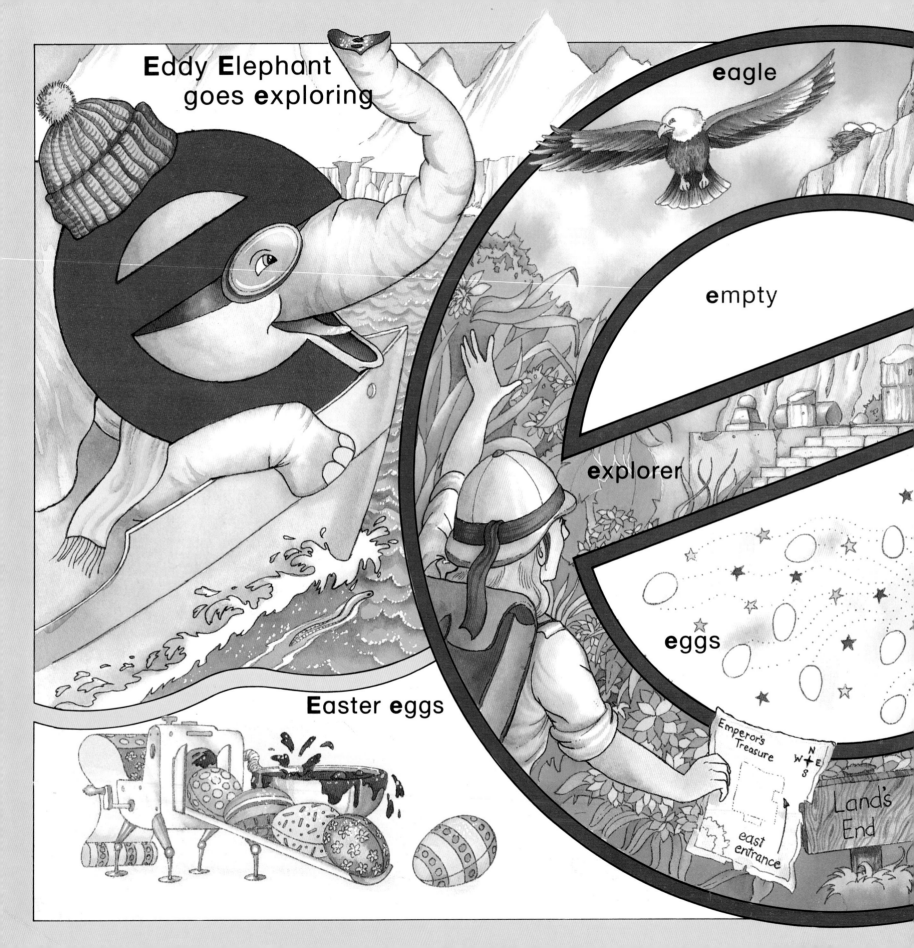

Eddy **E**lephant
goes **e**xploring

eagle

empty

explorer

eggs

Easter **e**ggs

Emperor's
Treasure

east
entrance

Land's
End

envelope

E. Elephant
11 Elmtree Estate
Letterland

escalator

entrance

EXIT

explosion

Mr E the
Easy
Magic
Man

Eddy **E**lephant
eating **e**clairs

Ee

Find the word

eclairs	**e**ntrance
Eddy	**e**nvelope
eggs	**e**scalator
Elephant	**E**state
Elm	**EXIT**
Elmtree	**e**xplorer
Emperor	**e**xploring
empty	**e**xplosion
End	

Mr **E**

eagle	**E**asy
east	**e**ating
Easter	

Activities

Add up all the eggs.

Find whose treasure is on the map.

Find the hidden eel.

Fireworks with Fireman Fred

fireflies in the forest

funny face on a flag

factory

fields

fence

fox

fern

football

frog

fork

FIRST AID

fifty pence

Ff

fire engine

frog

farm

farmer

Find the word

face	**F**ireworks
factory	**F**IRST AID
farm	**f**lag
farmer	**f**ootball
fence	**f**orest
fern	**f**ork
fields	**f**ox
fifty pence	**F**red
fire engine	**f**rog
fireflies	**f**unny
Fireman	**F**ulham

Activities

Count the fireflies.

Count the foxes in the field.

Find a hidden fish.

guitar

goal

gate

grapes

glider

garage

garden

goggles

grass

gloves

game

Golden **G**irl's
greenhouse

glass

glasses

gorilla

granny and **g**randad

goat **g**razing

goose

ghost

go kart

Gg

Find the word

game	**g**oggles
garage	**g**o kart
garden	**G**olden
gate	**g**oose
ghost	**g**orilla
Girl	**g**randad
glass	**g**ranny
glasses	**g**rapes
glider	**g**rass
gloves	**g**razing
goal	**g**reenhouse
goat	**g**uitar

Activities

Count the animals.

Find the grasshopper.

Find the green grapes.

The **H**airy **H**at Man at **h**ome

hatstand

Home Sweet Home

hair

hand

hill

hamburger

honey

hat

helmet

horse

hay

holly

HOTEL

Hilltop Hotel

hippo

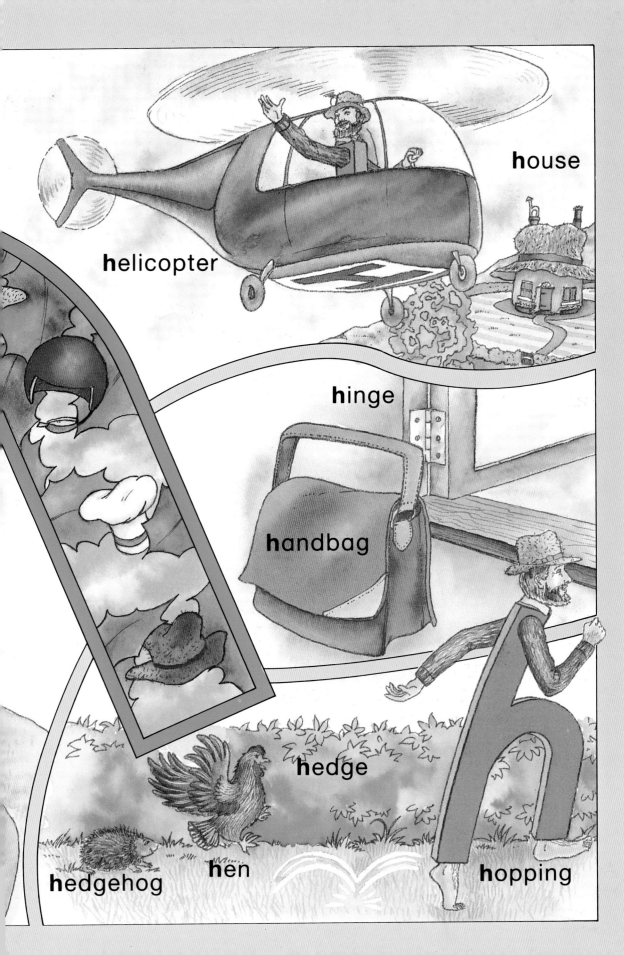

house

helicopter

hinge

handbag

hedge

hedgehog

hen

hopping

Hh

Find the word

hair	**h**ill
Hairy	**H**illtop
hamburger	
hand	**h**inge
handbag	**h**ippo
hat	**h**olly
hatstand	**h**ome
hay	**h**oney
hedge	**h**opping
hedgehog	**h**orse
helicopter	**H**OTEL
helmet	**h**ouse
hen	

Activities

Find the hammer.

Find the hidden hippo.

Count the hats.

Find all the helmets.

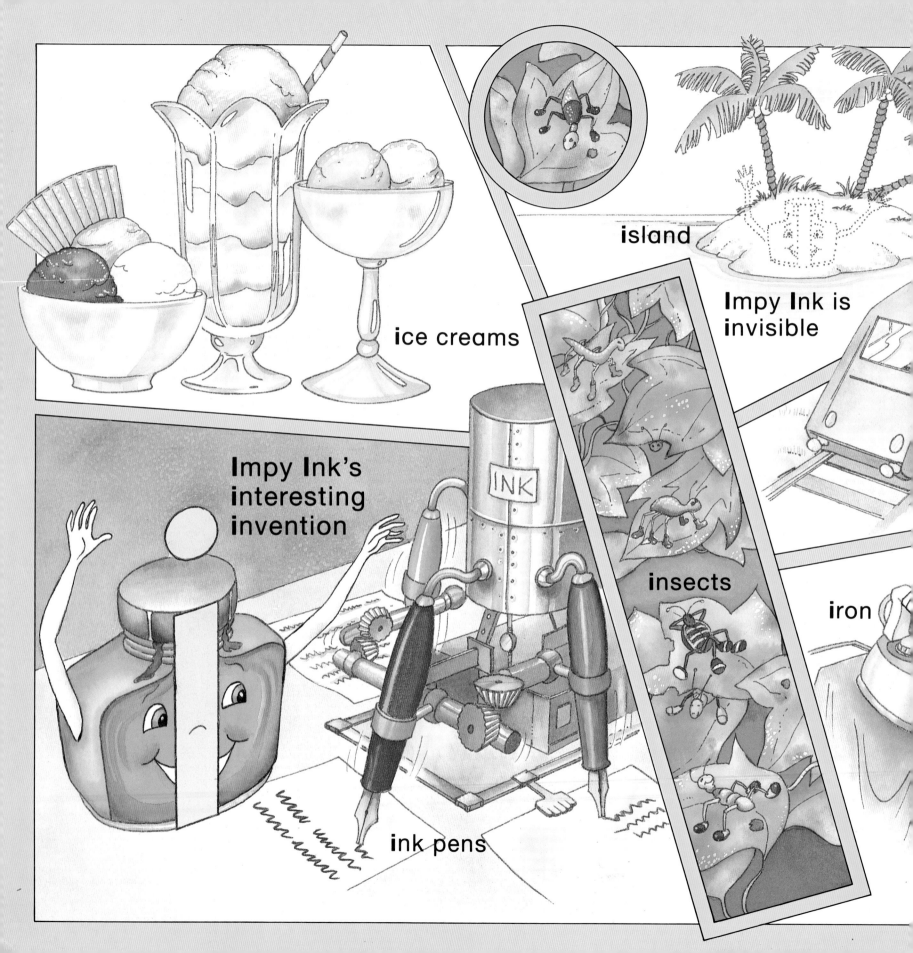

ice creams

island

Impy Ink is invisible

Impy Ink's interesting invention

insects

iron

ink pens

ill

intercity train

igloo

ice skating

invitation

Mr I the Ice Cream Man

Find the word

igloo	interesting
ill	invention
Impy	invisible
Ink	invitation
ink pens	is
insects	
intercity train	

Mr I
ice creams
ice skating
iron
island

Activities

Count the insects.

Count all the ice creams.

Find the invisible islander.

Dear Impy
Please come
to my party
on
Friday
love from
Mr I

jelly fish

Jumbo **j**et

jewels

jug

jeep

jaguars in the jungle

Find the word

jacket	jigsaw
jaguars	**J**im
jam	joke book
jars	joker
jeans	judge
jeep	jug
jellies	juggling
jelly	**J**umbo
jelly fish	**J**umping
jet	jumping
jewels	jungle

Activities

Count the juggling balls.

Find the hidden jelly.

Find the jack-in-the-box.

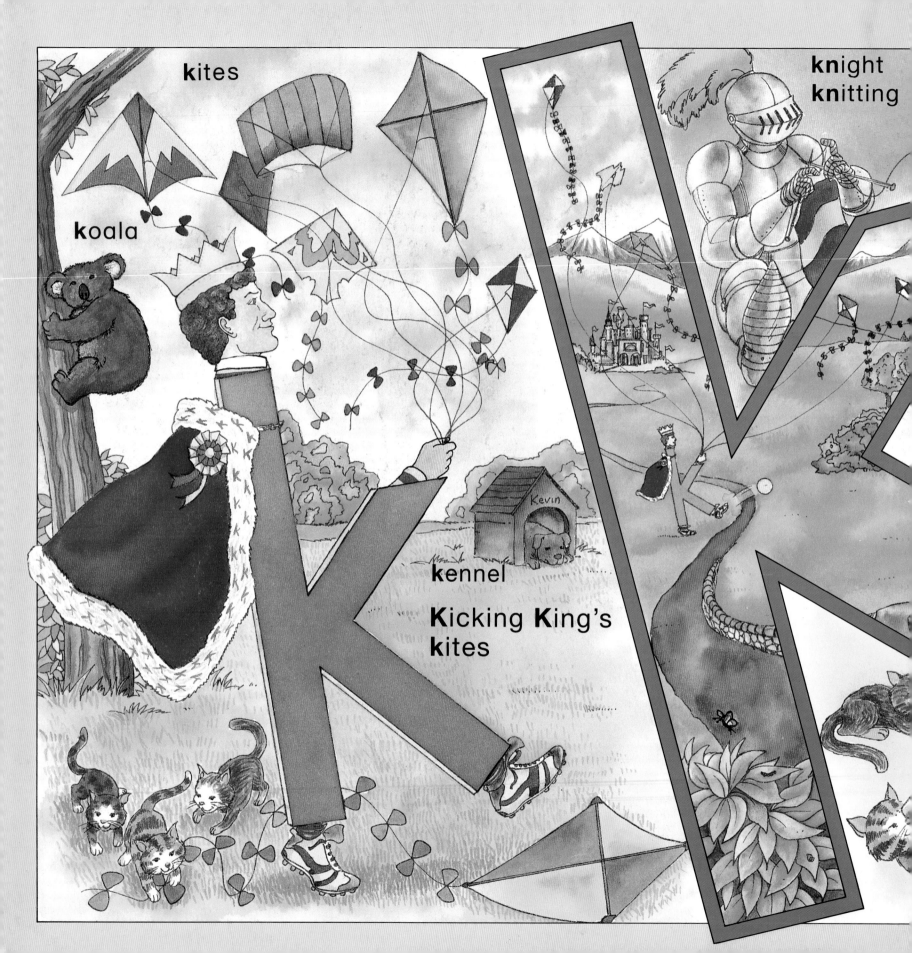

kites

koala

knennel

knight
knitting

Kicking **K**ing's
kites

Kevin

kitchen

kettle

ketchup

key

1 kilometre to the Kingdom

kangaroos
kissing

kittens

Kk

Find the word

kangaroos
kennel   **k**ingdom
ketchup   **k**issing
kettle   **k**itchen
Kevin   **k**ites
key   **k**ittens
Kicking   **kn**ight
King   **kn**itting
kilometre   **k**oala

Activities

Find two keys.

Count the kittens.

Count the kites.

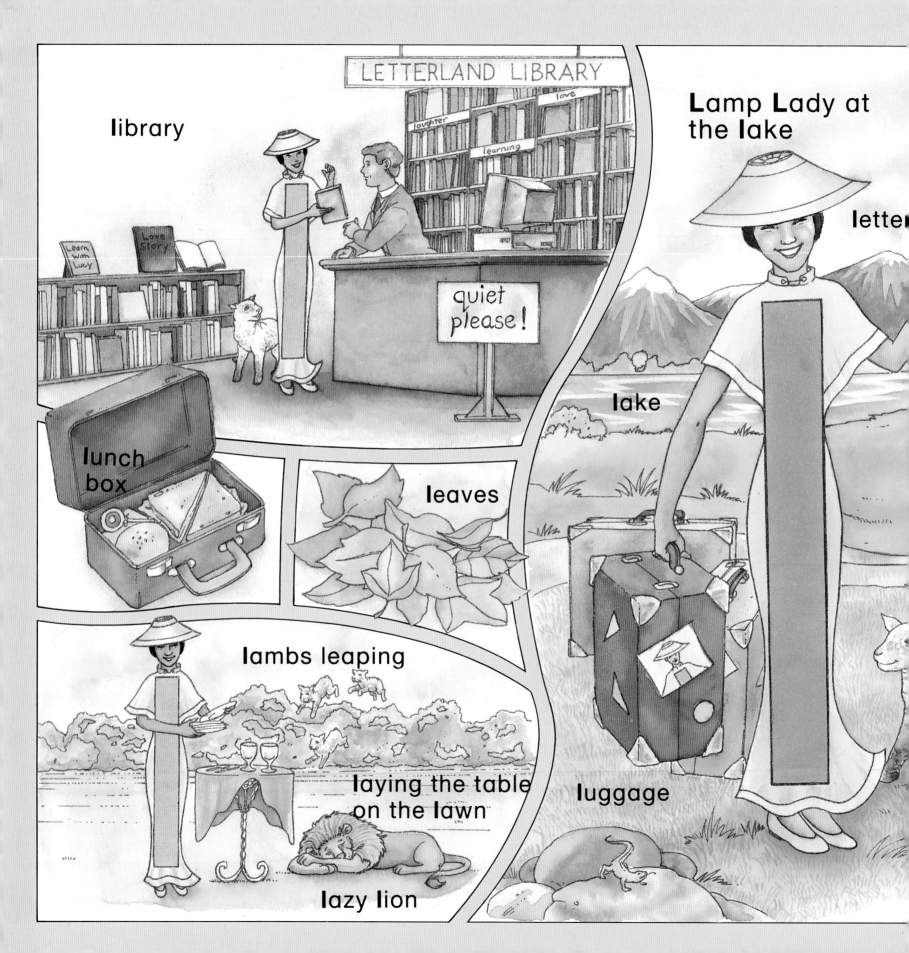

lemons

lightning

lighthouse

logs

ladder

lamb

lifeboat

light
lunch
lettuce
lemon
lime juice

lesson

Len's Leeks

lorry

Find the word

ladder
Lady
lake
lamb
Lamp
lawn
laying
lazy
leaves
Leeks
lemon
Len
lesson
LETTERLAND

lettuce
library
lifeboat
light
lighthouse
lightning
lime
lion
logs
lorry
luggage
lunch box

Activities

Find the lizard.

Count all the lambs.

Look for a lollipop.

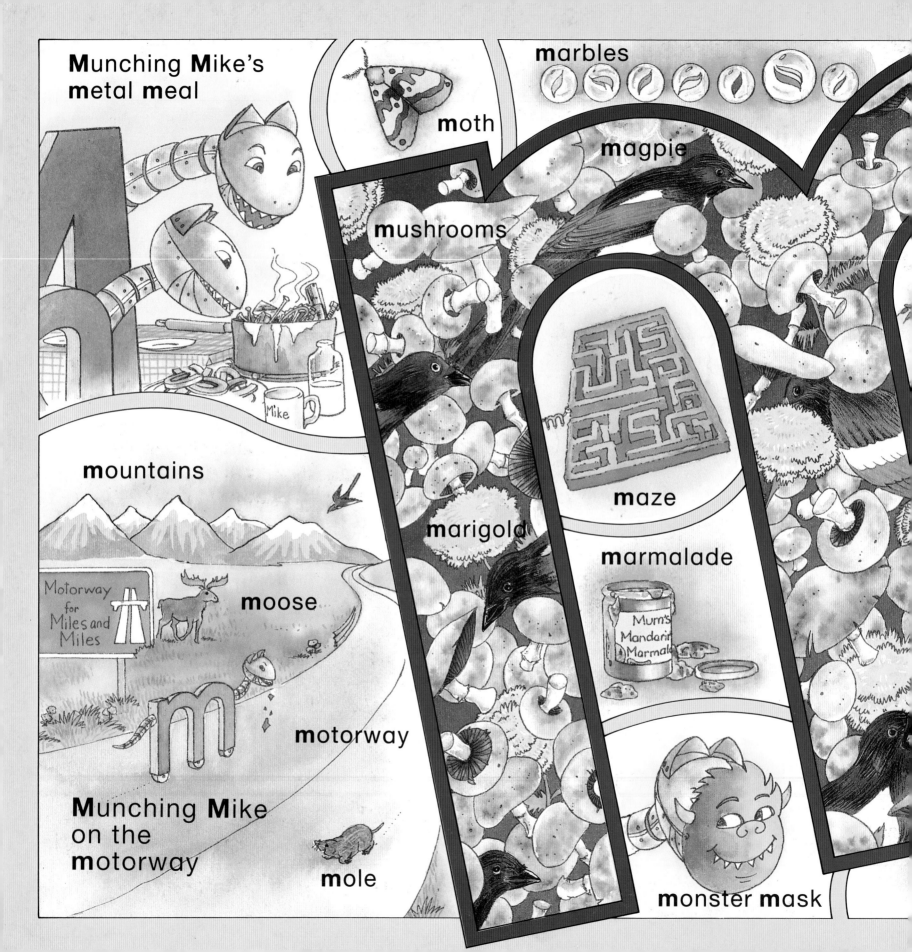

Munching **M**ike's **m**etal **m**eal

moth

marbles

magpie

mushrooms

mountains

moose

maze

marigold

marmalade

Motorway for Miles and Miles

Mike

Mum's Mandarin Marmalade

motorway

Munching **M**ike on the **m**otorway

mole

monster **m**ask

map

monkey

Misty Mountains

Motorway

Museum

Market

magic
mirror

model

microphone

music

motorbike

M m

Find the word

magic	**m**odel
magpie	**m**ole
Mandarin	**m**onkey
map	**m**onster
marbles	**m**oose
marigold	**m**oth
market	**m**otorbike
marmalade	
mask	**m**otorway
maze	**m**ountains
meal	**M**um
metal	**M**unching
microphone	
Mike	**M**useum
Miles	**m**ushrooms
mirror	**m**usic
Misty	

Activities

Count the magpies.

What is in Munching Mike's meal?

nest

No Entry

No Cycling

Notices

number nine

Naughty Nick's
newspaper

No More Noise say Nick's neighbours

noisy

neighbours

nails

needle

night

nurse

Nn

Find the word

nails	**n**ine
Naughty	**N**o
needle	**N**oise
neighbours	
nest	**n**oisy
net	**N**otices
News	**n**umber
newspaper	
Nick	**n**urse
night	**n**uts
nightly	

Activities

Find the hidden nightingale.

Add up all the nails.

Find the necklaces.

Count all the nests.

oranges

Oscar **O**range
over the **o**cean

one
o'clock

On or
off?

olives

Mr **O**

otter

octopus

office

Mr. O's office

open

ostrich

Find the word

octopus	**O**range
off	**o**ranges
office	**O**scar
olives	**o**strich
On	**o**tter

Mr **O**	**o**pen
ocean	**o**ver
o'clock	**o**verseas

Activities

Add up all the oranges.

How many legs on one octopus?

Which orange is the odd one out?

pencil

pennies

pears

Poor **P**eter and the **p**ostman

piano

postbox

penguins

postman with **p**arcels

palm trees

puddle

paws

parrot

pirate

pig

poppies

picture

puppet
painting

purple **p**aint

pony

pond

playground

Private

picnic

policeman

paper

plane

panda

present

Find the word

paint	**p**ig
painting	**p**irate
palm trees	**p**lane
Pam	**p**layground
panda	**p**oliceman
paper	**p**ond
parcels	**p**ony
parrot	**P**oor
paws	**p**oppies
pears	**p**ostbox
pencil	**p**ostman
penguins	**p**resent
pennies	**P**rivate
Peter	**p**uddle
piano	**p**uppet
picnic	**p**urple
picture	

Activities

Find all the presents.

What are the
penguins playing?

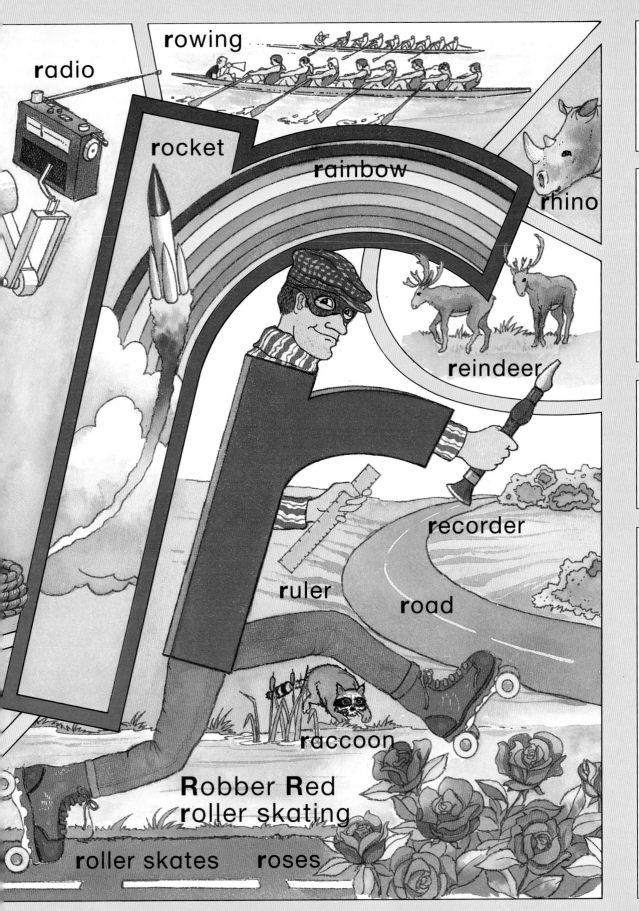

radio

rowing

rocket

rainbow

rhino

reindeer

recorder

ruler

road

raccoon

Robber **R**ed
roller skating

roller skates   **r**oses

Find the word

quads	**qu**iet
quail	**qu**ill
Quarrelsome **Qu**een	
quarters	**qu**ilt
question	**qu**iver

raccoon	**r**ob
radio	**R**obber
rainbow	**r**obot
recorder	**r**ocket
Red	**r**oller skates
reindeer	**r**ope
return	**r**oses
rhino	**r**owing
ring	**r**uler
road	**r**un

Activities

Find the reeds

Count the roses.

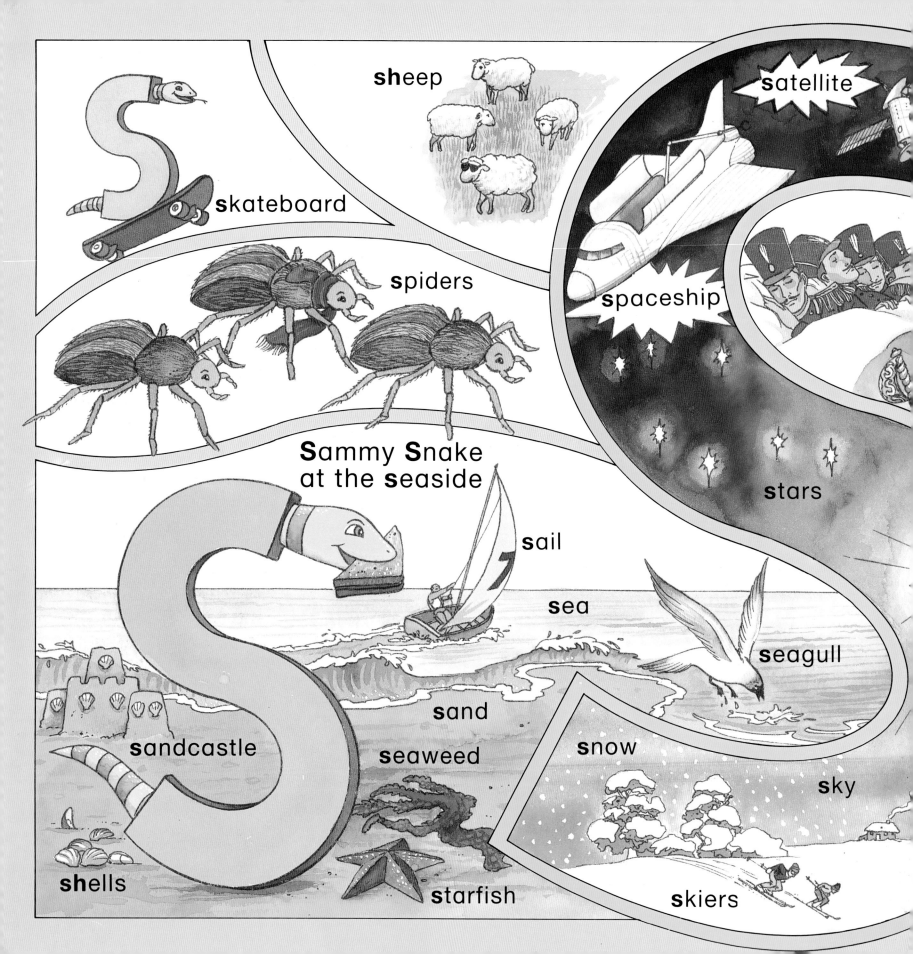

sheep

satellite

skateboard

spiders

spaceship

stars

Sammy **S**nake
at the **s**easide

sail

sea

seagull

sand

sandcastle

seaweed

snow

sky

shells

starfish

skiers

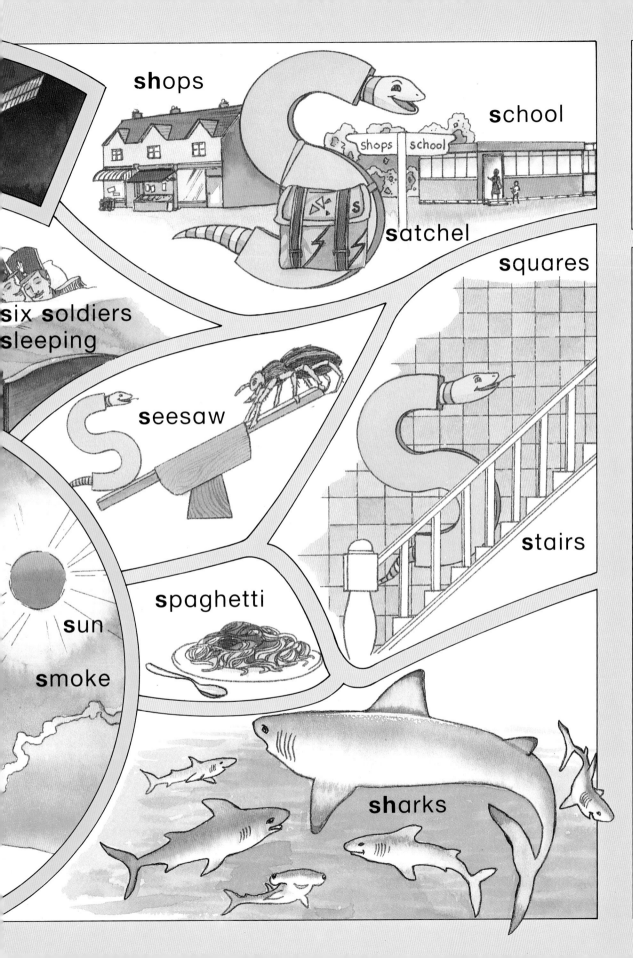

shops

school

satchel

squares

six soldiers **s**leeping

seesaw

stairs

spaghetti

sun

smoke

sharks

Ss

Find the word

sail	**s**kateboard
Sammy	**s**kiers
sand	**s**ky
sandcastle	**s**leeping
satchel	**s**moke
satellite	**S**nake
school	**s**now
sea	**s**oldiers
seagull	**s**paceship
seaside	**s**paghetti
seaweed	**s**piders
seesaw	**s**quares
sharks	**st**airs
sheep	**st**arfish
shells	**st**ars
shops	**s**un
six	**s**word

Activities

Count the sharks.

Find the sword.

Add up all the stars.

tiger

train

two tents

taxi

toothbrush

tissue

tap

toothpaste

typewriter

teddy bear

towel

TT

television

toys

tomatoes

Ticking Tess on the telephone

tape recorder

tortoise

ten tadpoles

trees

teapot

tractor

table

target

Ticking Tom

toadstools

Find the word

table	toadstools
tadpoles	Tom
tap	tomatoes
tape recorder	
target	toothbrush
taxi	toothpaste
teapot	tortoise
teddy bear	
telephone	towel
television	toys
ten	tractor
tents	train
Tess	trees
Ticking	two
tiger	typewriter
tissue	

Activities

Count the tomatoes.

Find three tortoises.

Find the traffic lights.

Find the trampoline.

up

Uppy **U**mbrella
upstairs

unicorn

Mr **U** the
Uniform Man

unhappy

umpire

umbrellas

underneath

volcano

vulture with
a violin

vines

viaduct

Vase of
Violets

valley

van

Uu

Find the word

umbrellas	**u**p
umpire	**U**ppy
underneath	**u**pstairs
unhappy	

Mr **U**   **U**niform Man
unicorn

Find the word

valley	**V**ince
van	**v**ines
Vase	**v**iolets
Vegetables	**v**iolin
Vet	**v**isitors
viaduct	**v**olcano
village	**v**ulture

Activities

Add up the umbrellas.

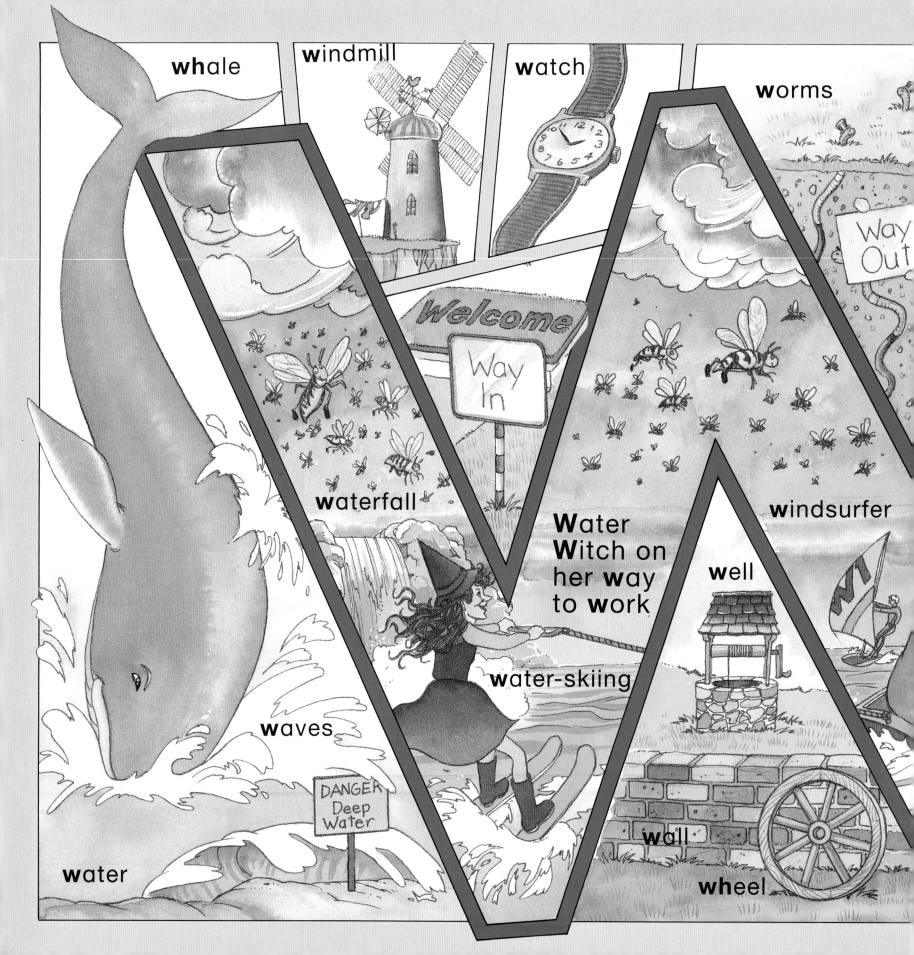

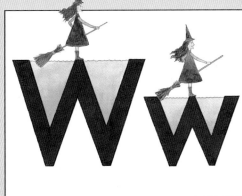

W w

wood

wolf

wasps

walrus

washing machine

Wet Wild Wash Wash Woollies

wool

wellington boots

Find the word

wall	Wet
walrus	whale
Wash	wheel
washing machine	
wasps	Wild
watch	windmill
Water	windsurfer
waterfall	Witch
water-skiing	
waves	wolf
way	wood
Way In	wool
Way Out	Woollies
Welcome	work
well	worms
wellington boots	

Activities

What is the Water Witch washing?

Who is the wolf waiting for?

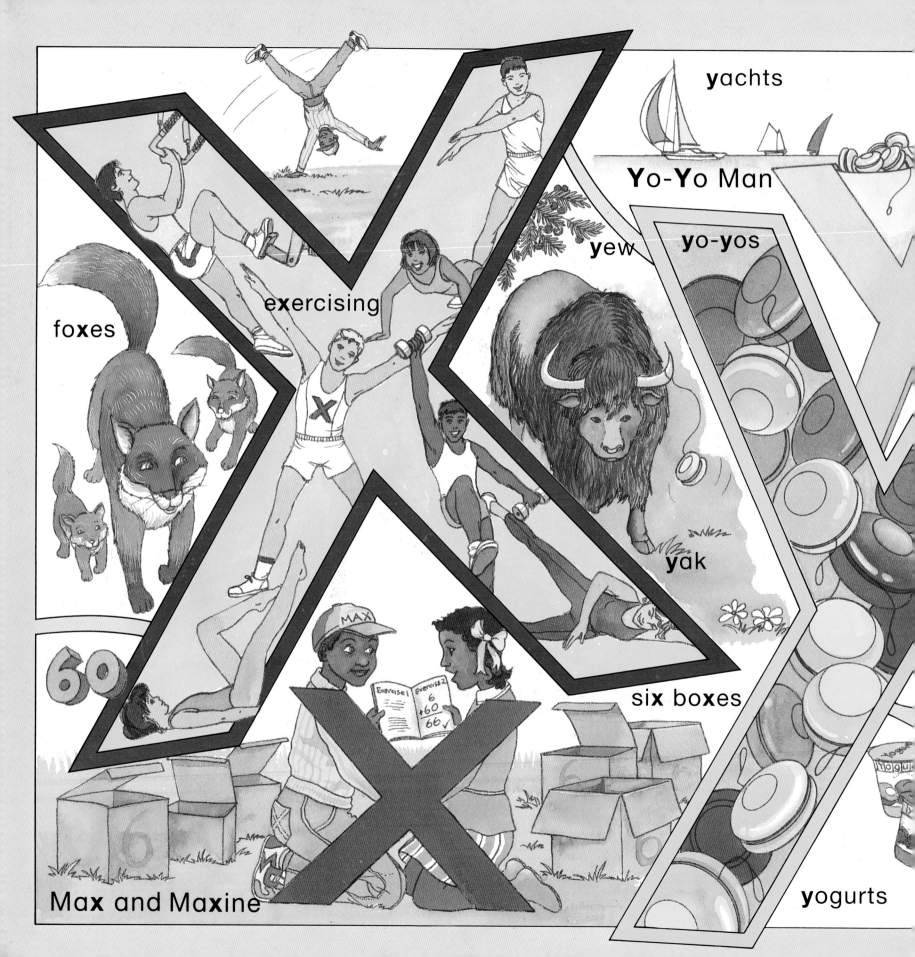

foxes

exercising

yachts

Yo-**Y**o Man

yew

yo-yos

yak

six bo**x**es

Ma**x** and Ma**x**ine

yogurts

zoo

Zig
Zag
Zebra

zebra crossing

zip

Find the word

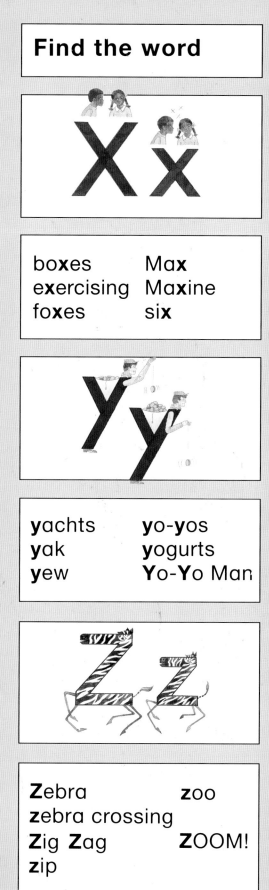

boxes   Max
exercising   Maxine
foxes   six

yachts   yo-yos
yak   yogurts
yew   Yo-Yo Man

Zebra   zoo
zebra crossing
Zig Zag   ZOOM!
zip

one camera

two kites

three jam jars

four hens

five nests

six lambs

seven Easter eggs

nine mushrooms

eight apples

ten bouncy balls

This book is dedicated to Alexander Carlisle — R.H.C.

Letterland Direct Ltd, PO Box 161, Leatherhead, Surrey KT2 3YB

First published by Letterland Direct Limited.

Copyright © The Templar Company plc 1992.

Letterland © was devised by and is the copyright of Lyn Wendon..
LETTERLAND® is a registered trademark.

Devised and produced by The Templar Company plc, Dorking, Surrey.

Illustrations created by Arkadia Ltd, London.
Edited by Lyn Wendon, Amanda Wood and Ian Tabor.

ISBN 1-85834-100-0

Colour separations by Positive Colour Ltd, Maldon, Essex.

Printed and bound in Italy